THE JEWEL IN THE CAVE

A Silver Medallion Novella

JOHN MOSS

This is a work of fiction. Names, characters, places, and incidents are products of the author's imagination or are used fictitiously and are not to be construed as real. Any resemblance to actual events, locations, organizations, or persons, living or dead, is entirely coincidental.

World Castle Publishing, LLC
Pensacola, Florida
Copyright © John Moss 2018
Paperback ISBN: 9781629899268
eBook ISBN: 9781629899275
First Edition World Castle Publishing, LLC, May 21, 2018
http://www.worldcastlepublishing.com
Licensing Notes
All rights reserved. No part of this book may be used or reproduced in any manner whatsoever without written permission, except in the case of brief quotations embodied in articles and reviews.
Cover: Karen Fuller
Editor: Maxine Bringenberg

Table of Contents

Chapter 1	5
Chapter 2	12
Chapter 3	20
Chapter 4	27
Chapter 5	36
Chapter 6	39
Chapter 7	45
Chapter 8	47
Chapter 9	52
Chapter 10	55
Chapter 11	65
Chapter 12	69
Chapter 13	73
Chapter 14	78
Chapter 15	85
Chapter 16	89

Chapter 17	99
Chapter 18	102
Chapter 19	112
Chapter 20	116
Chapter 21	125
Chapter 22	130
Chapter 23	136

Chapter 1

She could not feel the rope tied to her ankles. If the dark narrow burrow she was worming her way through became blocked or too cramped, she would use it to signal her companions and be dragged out, feet first—not a dignified exit, but Angel Harris seldom worried about dignity. And sometimes she discovered relics of ancient ancestors no one had seen for thousands upon thousands of years.

The surrounding limestone pressed on her from all sides. Rough edges dug into her shoulders. High overhead was the mountainous countryside of southern France; here was impenetrable darkness and rock. The tunnel was low, forcing her to tilt her head so the light on her helmet illuminated the opening ahead. Then she had to lower it again until her face scraped against silt and rubble as she blindly drew herself into the mysterious unknown.

Being born without the use of her legs gave Angel Harris certain advantages. She became an excellent swimmer, a wheelchair runner, and she could arm-wrestle men with bewildering success. Most importantly, her special abilities meant she could worm her way through impossibly small passages. Pulling herself along underground with the strength of her upper body, she went places others didn't dare. Her knack for dealing with her own fears as well as confined spaces had defined who she became: a specialist in cave-dwelling humans so ancient their bones had turned into stone.

She knew at least one person had been in this tunnel before. Her lamp picked up images on the rock of handprints outlined with faded red paint. The hands were small, each print the same size. One person. An older child? No, she thought, a young woman. Fifteen, sixteen? Half my age. Old enough to explore on her own, young enough to be fearless.

Fifty thousand years ago, this low narrow burrow might have seemed larger. The people were smaller. There would have been more room, perhaps only a few inches, but enough to allow the young woman to slide along with her pot of red paint, marking her way. Why? She couldn't get lost; there must be a small cavern ahead. How else would she have turned around? Was there something magical about her subterranean journey, something magical at the end to share with a disabled explorer, with two thousand generations between them?

Finally, Angel lifted her head and saw only darkness, not rock. The limestone had opened into a shapeless void. She squirmed forward and found herself in a cavern the size of a kitchen. Her suppressed fears drained away. She untied the safety rope from her ankles. She removed her headlamp from her helmet and cast its beam across the chamber floor. There were footprints. Oh my God, she thought. The young women's footprints! Nothing had disturbed their shapes in the dust. It was as if time had collapsed. The fearless young woman might have disappeared into the shadows just moments ago.

Angel raised the light beam to scan the walls. She was struck breathless. Painted on the contours of rock—hurtling toward her, running in front of her, filling the air of the cavern, clattering through cracks in the rock and through shadows—were bison and aurochs, a mammoth, a hippo, a horse, a saber-toothed cat. Creature after creature sprang into life.

And beneath the living stone, there were handprints outlined in black on the wall. The young woman's and a larger print, her partner's perhaps, two smaller prints, and barely visible, two more prints, very tiny, no more than scratch-marks etched into the rock. Here was a family picture unlike any that had been discovered before.

The Jewel in the Cave

Such a find was special. Angel was oddly happy that her smartphone couldn't connect her to the others from so deep in the limestone depths of the earth. She didn't want to diminish her experience by sharing. She didn't want to violate the timeless privacy of this primeval family, or turn the young woman's wondrous vision into a scientific artifact.

She needed to get closer to examine the paintings. She wanted to see the artist's handiwork close up, to dispel the illusion these animals were real. There were rock slides along the cavern walls, small boulders and rubble shaken free when the Earth was much younger. This gave her a rough ledge to work her way across, without disturbing the footprints. When she was so close to the handprints she could have touched them, the crawling platform narrowed precariously. She had to boost herself up so see better. She slipped and tumbled into the silt.

Horrified that she had altered the scene, which had not been disturbed since time immemorial, she carefully placed one hand beneath her and reached for a grip with the other, to haul herself back onto the rough ledge. As she did so, her fingers in the silt closed on a smooth object. Instinctively, she grasped it.

Once secure, with only the impression of her body on the floor to mark her violation of what, as a scientist and as a person, she felt was a sacred sight, she surveyed the scene from her different perspective. The fine texture of the area she had fallen into suggested the dust left from reeds or skins, not rocks. Organic matter. This must have been the girl's bed; she had slept here while she worked. A blackened circle of small rocks nearby showed where there had been fires for light and for warmth. Everywhere, there were imprints of bared human feet. Mostly they were the girl's, although a path of the man and two children's cut directly across from the tunnel exit to the painted wall and back again. The man's were deep on the way in, as if he had been carrying something heavy.

These details were exciting. They would

have to be properly documented. She would use her smartphone for now, but return with a proper camera to record them, to record everything. This made her both happy and sad. She could never capture the awesome experience of discovery, when all that lay between her and the young woman was time.

She reached for her camera in her side pocket and realized she was still clutching the smooth stone she had found in the silt. Again, she was horrified at having disturbed the scene. But here it was, now, the stone in her hand. She would photograph exactly where she had found it.

She lifted it to the light, blew dust away, gently polished it against her sleeve, and gazed into the depths of an ancient gem of syrup that had hardened through millions of years into an amber jewel. Oh my God! Angel slouched against the rocks, wanting to hold this moment forever.

Chapter 2

The fearless young woman was not fearless at all. Fear allowed humans to survive in a perilous world. She had to know when to run, when to fight, when to hide. She had to know when to be quiet and when to make noise. She never let fear control her; she controlled her fears. She was strong willed and serene, as if she were fearless.

When she approached the strangers, she was exhausted and hungry. She had no fear. They were humans like her, although her hair was auburn, a reddish-brown, and theirs was black, and her face was a little different, with stronger features. Some of them wore animal skins over their shoulders and a sash of leather draped from their waists. Most were covered in layers of mud and animal grease to protect them from insects and the blazing sun.

She extended her hand in a gesture of peace, clenching her fingers into a fist, then spreading them with her palm opened in their direction. These others smiled with bared teeth; she bared her own teeth in return.

Behind them, shelters made from skins indicated a community of no more than five or six families. The skins on the shelters had been scraped free of hair and then smoked, before the oils of crushed animal brains were rubbed in to make the leather waterproof. The cured skins were stretched over poles leaning against a rock wall. In extreme weather, the people would retreat to nearby caves which were cooler in summer, easier to keep warm in winter.

Her own people lived much the same way, in shelters and caves. Like these strangers, they mostly used auroch skins. Aurochs were slow and clumsy cattle, with long horns and shaggy coats. In the cold, their skins were used with the hair still on them, to cover the people huddled beside open fires.

The young woman walked into the center of the camp. There were no men in sight, only a few small boys. The women poked at her to make sure she was real. Smaller children kept their distance but the older children teased her with sticks. She stared straight ahead. The women slapped the older children away and stopped poking. They made chattering sounds among themselves, then to her.

She remained silent, then responded with gestures.

Even among themselves, these humans did not have language; they did not have words. Nor did the young woman. She pointed to the foothills in the distance, then to herself, and placed an open hand over her heart before tapping her chest with one finger. Suddenly reaching away, she nervously fluttered her fingers. Her family, her loved ones, were gone. Her eyes expressed stress and confusion. They had fled or been killed. With a single finger she again jabbed at her heart. She was alone.

What happened? they asked by holding hands upright, palms outward. The rhythm of their chatter became more intense. They tried to understand.

The young woman stood silent and still. There was nothing more to convey. She had no idea where her people had gone. She had spent days deep in a cave, and when she emerged from the depths of the earth they were gone.

Every single person in her world had vanished. She had not cried then. Despite mounting despair, she refused to cry now, in front of strangers.

She glared at the people around her. They were like her, but they were not her own people. How could they understand the depths of her loneliness?

Several men approached from a distance, carrying huge chunks of bleeding meat. They had killed a woolly mammoth.

Joy and grief filled the air. The hunt had been successful. There would be a feast. But nine men had gone out and only seven returned. There would be sadness.

The young woman understood all this by reading the gestures and expressions of the people. The returning hunters ignored the stranger. She was alone — she posed no threat.

The men took slices of chipped stone from folds in the animal skins around their waists. They cut away handfuls of meat and gave them to the women in exchange for leaf bowls loaded with berries. Without ceremony, their feast began. Some ate the meat raw, others threaded bite-sized bits on sticks and held them over the glowing coals of a very small fire. The fire snapped and sizzled as fat melted into the sparkling embers.

A young hunter handed the fearless young woman a piece of raw meat. She sat on a stone and tore at the meat with her teeth. She popped handfuls of berries into her mouth, then wiped away purple stains on her lips with the back of her hand.

After they finished eating, an old woman squatted in front her and held up a large piece of amber, the size of an egg yolk and the color of flowing honey. The young woman took the gem in her hand. She had never seen such a thing. It looked soft and warm, but was hard and cool to the touch. It had edges and planes that carried reflections, but at the same time it had depths, as if it contained worlds within.

She turned it and saw a distorted image of her own face. Startled, she dropped the gem onto the stone beneath her.

It cracked and split evenly into two pieces.

She picked up one piece of amber, the old woman the other. They each held their pieces toward the sun, which was low on the horizon. Light poured through and washed across their faces. The young woman closed her fist on her amber disc and squeezed so firmly the edges cut into her skin. Then she faced away from the sun and turned it this way and that until a girl's face reappeared on the flat surface where it had split. Flashing white teeth. Hazel eyes. Tangled reddish-brown hair. Skin caked with mud. She muttered a single sound.

"Mee."

The old woman smiled and repeated her word. "Me."

The young woman frowned. "Me," she repeated, pointing to herself.

The old woman took the amber from her. She stood up and uttered loud sounds until she had the attention of their entire small group.

She pointed to the fearless young woman. "ME," she said.

The young woman repeated the sound, emphatically then quietly. "ME-me."

No one had ever used a sound pattern like that to carry a single meaning. In her own mind, and in theirs, she had become a word.

The old woman handed the amber back to the clever young woman. It was hers to keep.

By nightfall the grownups had given themselves names, which most of them soon forgot. The children gave themselves several. A solemn name, a giggle name, and a secret name known only to themselves.

Chapter 3

Angel reached into the side pocket of her coveralls. Her fingers closed around the one thing in her life she treasured most—a silver medallion that had been in her family for generations. There was a gaping hole in the center, the color of tarnished silver, where a piece of amber had once been embedded. Her mother, Sophie, had explained when she gave it to her that the amber had turned to dust in a terrible fire. The chain snagged on Angel's clothes as she tugged the medallion free. Rolling onto her side, she wriggled herself upright, then she relaxed her grasp on the amber jewel she'd found in the silt. With the helmet back on her head and the lamp attached, she directed the cone of light on the two objects she held side by side. One hazel eye and one gaping grey eye gazed back at her without blinking.

She felt badly for removing the amber from where it had rested in the silt for thousands of years. It would be fake to replace it and pretend it hadn't been moved. She decided to take it out with her. It would eventually go to a museum, either at home or in France. She needed a way to keep it safe on her return journey through the tunnel.

A jewel of time-frozen sap gleaming in the palm of her hand, it felt strangely familiar. She lay it over the tarnished hole in her silver medallion again, twisted and pressed hard. It clicked into place like it was meant to be there, like it had been waiting thousands of years to be found.

A strange feeling crept over her, as if she had crawled into another dimension where the past was more real than the present. She gazed around at the colors and shadows and contours of the cavern. The painted stone was more real than its witness. The young woman's world seemed more real than her own.

Directly across from her a bison shuddered. When she looked up, the bison was still. She looked away — it shuddered again. Its muscles tightened, preparing for flight. From the shadows, the saber-toothed cat, caught by the artist leaping to attack, screamed with excitement. The mammoth, the auroch, a horse, and a flock of birds snorted, whinnied, and murmured in a riot of noise.

And suddenly the walls became still. There was silence.

The cavern was empty until Angel awoke with a start.

She hadn't planned to sleep. The others would be worried about her. They were scientists, like herself. They had lots to explore in the cavern where they had made camp, although none of them would have dared to enter the low narrow tunnel to find this special place. She checked the time. Ninety minutes had passed since she had arrived, two and a half hours since she had left camp. She would need a full hour to return.

It was time to leave. She moved carefully around the edge of the cavern, taking pictures. A warning light showed her battery was almost gone. Since the phone wouldn't work at these depths, she continued photographing until the unit went dead. Then she wriggled around to the opening of the tunnel and attached the end of the safety rope to her belt.

Angel gave a sharp tug on the rope. There were markers on it that told her how far she was from the others. One hundred and eighty meters. Or yards. The markers weren't very accurate. She tugged again. There was no response. The rope must have jammed between rocks. Pulling it taut, grasping it firmly, she gave another, more powerful tug.

The rope snapped free and lay slack in the silt. Angel picked it up tentatively and pulled. It came toward her with no resistance. It was no longer connected to her companions. She was no longer connected to the surface of the world.

Anxious about having to squirm back with no safety line, Angel was also puzzled and angry. Surely they would have tied the end down. Her life depended on it. Now it was beyond their reach.

She hauled the entire length into the cavern. It wasn't worth the risk, worming her way back with it tangling beneath her. The markers were no longer of interest, and she knew how far she had come.

Boosting herself up against the wall, she balanced her medallion lightly in the palm of one hand. It had passed through generations of girls and women in her family, and gave her comfort that she wasn't alone. She gazed into the depths of the amber disc, connecting to the fearless young woman who had painted her visions in stone. It was as if the thousands and thousands of years between them collapsed.

As she squirmed around, preparing to exit, the light on her headlamp flickered and went out. Darkness closed around her like a burial shroud.

"My God, my God," she murmured.

The batteries should have lasted another twelve hours.

"My God, my God," she repeated. She wasn't praying. Angel didn't pray. But she wasn't swearing. "God, my God," simply summed up her feelings beyond words, feelings of absolute dread.

She touched her fingers to her face. She could feel them move through the air, but she could not see them. This was what blindness must be like. Not black, not a dazzling absence of light, just nothing at all.

Angel took a few deep breaths, until her rising panic subsided.

Maneuvering the medallion to her back, so it dropped between her shoulder blades inside her clothes, was reassuring. She needed to know it was there, but wanted to avoid crushing it against her flesh while creeping on her belly toward safety or into oblivion.

She wasn't sure which it would be. Safety or oblivion.

Angel smiled to herself, to the fearless young woman of the cave, and plunged forward into the darkness.

Chapter 4

With meat from the mammoth and plentiful berries, there was no pressure to hunt or gather. When the young woman had been wandering on her own, her mind was on the struggle to survive. Now she had time to think. Over the next few days, she stared at the foothills on the distant horizon. The more she went over in her mind what might have happened, the more upset she became.

She had been deeper in her family's cave than anyone else had ever dared to go. Crawling through a narrow tunnel, she had pushed ahead of her a piece of bone from the skull of an auroch. It was turned upside down and filled with animal fat, with a braid of dry reeds burning at one end, to provide light. She hauled behind her a sack with water in a large gourd that had been hollowed out and sealed with cork, and a bundle of dried meat, as well as an auroch skin to sleep on and a bag of rock powder to make orange-red paint when mixed with water or pee. On an earlier trip she had painted the outline of her hand along the tunnel wall to mark her way. This was not just an adventure through a crack in the earth; it was a journey into an unknown cavern within her own mind. She wanted to be sure she would find her way out.

She planned to paint her visions of the animals that haunted her dreams. She did not fear these animals. She needed to set them free, and was determined to stay until her painting was done.

Days later, when she emerged into the larger cave where her people lived, no one was there.

The Jewel in the Cave

Wary, worried, she stepped outside into the sunlight. There was no one.

She was alone. The mothers who had raised her, her fathers, her brothers and sisters, were gone. Had they left her behind and gone on some journey? Was it because she was different? Because the green in her eyes made them hazel, not brown. Because her skin was smoother, her hair more twisted and glistening, and reddish-brown, not black, or her nose was smaller, her chin more squared, her lips fuller, her teeth more even and perfectly shaped? She had no idea what she looked like, herself. Reflections in water were not to be trusted. Nor were images reflected in amber.

She could identify most of the footprints near the cave entrance with the person who'd made them. At this time of year, her family did not bind their feet with leather for protection. A few imprints indicated the presence of strangers. These were broad and flat, their depth suggesting the weight of large men.

There were no indications of a skirmish.

The skin coverings had been stripped from shelters close to the cliff, leaving bare poles. This suggested to her either a raid by strangers or methodical flight. She couldn't be sure. Were her people abducted, or did they simply move on without her?

Frantic and yet methodical, she searched for a spear and a fire-making kit made of folded leather with two small rocks inside, one of black flint and the other iron pyrite, which glittered like gold. Then she set out on a quest to find her family.

The wind had obliterated all signs of their passing. She wandered from one full moon to the next, drinking from streams and eating insects, thinking about feelings she couldn't express, thinking about being alone in the world.

Now she gazed at these people who had taken her in. Their kindness made her feel guilty. It was as if she had abandoned her family, not they who had abandoned her.

As day turned to night on her third day, she

sat close to the largest cave entrance. Despite the warm evening air, a fire smoldered nearby. It was smudged with green branches, making billows of smoke to keep the mosquitoes and blackflies away.

She removed the amber disc from her leather waistband. As she turned it in her hand, she saw her image amid flames licking out past the greens on the fire. She closed her fingers around the amber and clutched it so tightly it cut into her flesh. Then she released the pressure and held it lightly, as if to protect it. It was streaked with blood. It would be hers for two thousand generations.

Some girls MEme's age motioned with their hands to indicate she was welcome to join them inside, behind the curtain of smoke. As her eyes adjusted, she saw several girls bathing in a shallow pool beneath a small waterfall at the back of the cave. They used a mixture of ashes and water to scrub the greasy mud from their faces and bodies. Then each took spikes of lavender blossom and rolled the flowers into a paste between their palms. They rubbed the sweet-smelling paste over their glistening bodies as they lounged beside the pool.

She had never seen such behavior before but joined in their ritual, breathing deeply to enjoy the scent. For a few moments she forgot about everything.

She was happy to sit with her new friends, murmuring and giggling, safe in the cave, away from the insects.

"MEme," she said.

"MEme," said the others, and offered their own sound clusters, searching for patterns that pleased them.

One of the young women used gestures to ask her again where she came from. She waved to indicate far away, then she swept her hands downwards and scooped handfuls of silt into a pile. They looked puzzled. She cut across the top of the mound with an index finger, spread the silt aside and, touching her fingertips together as she reached into the depression, she drew out an imaginary infant and held it to her breast. She had been born out of the earth. Some gasped as the mythic nature of the story sank in; others laughed. Humans were born from a woman's body, not from beneath the ground. They quickly lost interest and returned to their lavender potions.

After a fitful sleep, MEme got up and walked out into the open. A young man her own age, a boy, stirred the embers of the fire. He was the young hunter who'd given her meat after they returned from the hunt. He added a few green twigs. He seemed to have been up most of the night.

His eyes widened but he did not smile. She walked past him and sat by herself.

Behind her she could hear people emerging from the cave and the shelters. She turned and watched them as they went about eating their morning meal. They had been kind to her, but they were strangers.

The boy walked over and stood beside her. Together they gazed toward the green hills of her home. He had washed mud and blood from his face and hands at the pool inside the cave, after the girls were finished. But he did not smell of lavender. The scent might scare animals away when he hunted. She looked into his eyes and her eyes filled with tears.

At home she was also a hunter. Here she would pick berries and care for the children.

She gazed across the shimmering grasslands.

She thought of her kin individually. There were enough of them that she could count them on her fingers and toes, if she had understood counting and numbers — but she did not. She missed them desperately.

She turned from the boy as she rose to her feet, angry he had seen her tears, and walked over to a stack of spears leaning against the rock wall by the cave's entrance. She selected one of medium length, then turned to the cache of meat laying in the shadows. Using her amber disc as a tiny knife she cut off a chunk, which she wrapped in a leather bandeau and bound to her waist.

The Jewel in the Cave

Without talking to anyone, not even the boy who had made her his friend, she clambered down the rocks and walked out into the grasslands in the direction she'd come from. She had found no evidence among these people that her family had passed this way. There was a vast unknown world to search, and she was filled with the overwhelming need to resolve the mystery of their disappearance, to find out why they had left her alone, to find out what happened to them—to find them, if they were abducted, and bring them home.

CHAPTER 5

Angel Harris worked her way inch by inch through darkness pressing in from all sides. It seemed like squirming in place, getting nowhere. She took a deep breath and reached blindly ahead, sinking her fingers into the rubble, pulling herself forward, holding her head so low her cheek scraped the rubble and silt. Edges of limestone cut into her shoulders. One arm dragged behind as she reached with the other. Lifting her head, squinting to keep the grit out of her eyes, she stared into the darkness without seeing. There was no way to be certain she was moving at all.

The Jewel in the Cave

She hovered on the edge of hysterical fear, not mindless but not thinking, trying to keep words from her mind as she imagined herself like the fearless young woman who had painted her vision in the cavern behind her. They were both part of the earth, the earth's mind, aware of itself.

Reaching ahead to clutch rubble, Angel's knuckles smashed against stone. She felt around; dead end. The tunnel was blocked. When she had yanked the safety rope, she had caused a rock-fall. The walls of the tunnel had collapsed. Or perhaps they had collapsed earlier and severed the line. She hadn't thought to check the markers to see if the rope was cut short.

She allowed herself to think. With her exit obstructed, she would soon, like the young woman, become dust. They would be the same, with no time between them. Their amber disc, clasped in a silver medallion, would remain, and slowly be buried in the silt and the rubble.

She smiled, knowing she would soon

become part of the earth. She was dying; the process had already begun.

CHAPTER 6

The young woman who called herself MEme kept her eyes on the horizon as she made her way through the underbrush, across an open plain and dried marshland. Shortly after the sun had passed its highest point in the sky, she spotted a flock of ravens circling just off her route. When she approached, they squawked and flew away, leaving behind the remains of a woolly mammoth.

When she got closer, she realized the bloody carnage included the corpses of two humans, the hunters who had not returned to their village the previous day. Their ribs were sticking through shredded skin and their eye sockets were empty. Their mouths gaped open where the ravens had plucked out their brains.

Gathering what remained of the men's bodies into a heap, she piled rocks around them and on top, and brushed furiously at the flies they attracted. When the job was almost done, movement in the undergrowth caught her attention. She crouched beside the cairn of boulders and gazed into the shadows in the direction of the noise. With one hand grasping her spear, the other balancing against the rocks, she was poised to spring when the creature attacked.

When there was no possibility of flight, there was no fear. She waited.

A shadow loomed over her, cast from the side. She sprang to her feet and, wheeling, thrust the spear in front of her.

The sharpened point stopped a handsbreadth from the chest of the boy, the young man who had tried to comfort her in front of the cave. He held his hands to his sides, showing he would not fight. But he stood tall. He would not submit.

She relaxed. He had followed her. Was he going to take her back? He could try! But he added a few rocks to the burial cairn to show that he was there to be with her, not take her captive. She lowered her spear but did not smile.

Digging into the mammoth remains with their hands, they discovered unspoiled meat which they devoured raw. They dried a few thin slabs in the sun, hoping vainly to prevent further rotting.

For the next six days they walked side by side. After she left her own cave, she had wandered aimlessly, dealing with loneliness and confusion. Now she was on a direct route home, guided by the contours of the horizon, by the changing vegetation and the colors of the soil, by shifting angles of sunlight through the days. She did not read these markers so much as sense them.

She was angry and determined. Angry that

she had lost her family. Determined to find them.

Discarding the remains of the rancid mammoth meat, they hunted ground squirrels and rabbits. Occasionally they chewed on dried crickets and beetles. They drank from streams flowing down from the hills. At night they huddled close to each other for comfort in darkness that teemed with dangerous sounds.

On the evening of their seventh day, she was in familiar territory.

Even though it was growing dark, she led the boy upwards until they came to a place where the earth had long ago been sheared away in a flood and the rock was exposed. They followed the rocky wall past deep clefts to a gorge with water running through it. They followed the stream upwards to a small plateau, where it disappeared into a wall of darkness and stone.

Poles leaned here and there against the rock face, all that was left of her family shelters.

The fearless young woman reached into a gap between some boulders and pulled out a clump of dry wood shavings. Before the boy could comprehend what she was doing, she removed small pieces of flint and iron pyrite from their folded leather packet, knelt down, struck the rocks to make sparks, and started a fire.

He had never seen flint being used before. In his family group they had long ago captured flames from a burning tree where lightning had struck. The fire in front of his family's cave had been burning all of his life.

Quickly they added sticks from a pile of gathered wood, and soon had a roaring blaze to protect them from darkness. They roasted the remains of a rabbit and ate, but, rather than settle down for the night, she insisted they make a torch from burning sticks and move into the darkness alongside the rock face. When it seemed there was nowhere further to go, a cleft leading off to the side opened into a large cavern. The torchlight glinted on the walls and he was amazed, but she seemed completely at home.

As their eyes grew accustomed to the dazzling play of shadows and light, they could see small scraps of skin and fur, and bits of wood and a fire pit made of stones in a circle, heaped with ashes from countless fires.

The young woman sank in despair to the dusty clay floor of the cave. The boy settled beside her. He raised the torch above their heads and gazed at the innumerable footprints around them. It would not have been difficult to imagine a family group much like his own, all living together in this cavern through the coldest days of winter. The stillness was frightening, the flickering shadows were teeming with ghosts.

It was a relief for both when the torch faded and turned from glowing embers to black. They fell asleep in each other's arms.

Chapter 7

Parched with thirst, her guts gnawing with hunger, Angel tried to escape into sleep. If she could die in her sleep, it would all be over. But she could not sleep. She was the mind of the earth being aware of itself.

Enough!

She had to stop such magical mystical thinking. Life was too rare, too precious not to be savored right to the end.

She thought of the time, years ago, when she and her friend Maddie had been the survivors of a plane crash in the northern wilderness of central Canada. Maddie was gravely injured.

Angel had crawled around in the snow, building a shelter, fueling a fire, snaring rabbits. It was perhaps the best time of her life.

I will endure until I am dead, she thought.

I will endure.

Chapter 8

Morning announced itself with a thin sliver of light shining between the boulders at the cave entrance. After a meal of berries collected nearby, MEme and the boy made another torch and returned to the cave.

She seemed to be searching, but didn't know what she was looking for. There were no stacks of fur, no auroch skins, no dried fish or meat, no gourds stained with grease, no bowls made of folded bark filled with dried fruit, and yet there were piles of wood. There were a few scraps of fur on the floor, a few gnawed bones by the fire.

She tried to make sense of this.

Her people had taken their food and coverings with them. They'd intended to travel, but they left the firewood behind. Why hadn't she thought of this before? They were headed north, where wood for fires was plentiful. She still was not sure whether they had set out on a great journey accompanied by the strangers with broad feet, or had been abducted.

A great journey took extensive planning. She would have known about it. But if raiders had descended on the camp without warning and taken them all away, and taken all their supplies, she would have known nothing of what had happened until she emerged from the ecstasies of painting in the subterranean depths.

She turned and, thrusting her torch ahead of her, she slid through a narrow crevasse near the back of the cavern. The boy reluctantly followed.

What had seemed no more than a fold in the rocks turned out to be a series of small caves which had been gouged out by swirling waters eons ago. Eventually, the caves opened into a dry stream bed, which they followed as it split off into a complicated network of passages. The young woman proceeded, confident of where she was leading.

She didn't seem worried that their torch was burning low. The boy finally put his hand on her shoulder to stop her. He pointed to the dwindling flame. He could tell by the cooling stillness of the air that they were not moving toward another entrance, they were moving deeper into the bowels of the earth. They would never find their way out without light.

He made unfamiliar sounds as if he were speaking another language. It was their harsh lack of harmony, muttered in soft tones, that indicated his concern.

She answered him in a melodious lilt with sounds of her own.

He smiled without showing his teeth. It was a gesture of trust. It was not a gesture of happiness.

They came to a small opening in the rock, a tunnel so small they could only move ahead if they crawled. Their torch flickered. She lit a small lamp made of an auroch skull. It had been sitting in a niche, waiting for her return. She cast the torch aside. It flared and sparked and went out.

The boy silently followed as they wormed their way through the rock. At last, they emerged into a cavern the size of two mammoths standing together. The young woman walked directly to a pile of sticks and used the lamp to start a fire. The cavern filled with smoke and then cleared as the fire blazed and a draft was created through fissures overhead that acted like a chimney.

The walls all around them gleamed in the light.

There was enough firewood to last for a week. There were caches of nuts in their shells and sun-dried fruits. She had completed her painting before her supplies had run out. Near one wall there was a pool fed by a trickle of fresh clean water. On the floor was straw bedding, and there were folded covers made of animal fur.

On the far wall, the flames revealed a series of unusual shapes. At first they appeared to be nothing more than planes and contours in the rock. Then as their eyes adjusted, colors appeared. Magnificent colors in the shapes of running animals, of bison and deer and horses and aurochs and mammoths and a saber-toothed cat.

MEme spread her arms out in front of the pictures. She was filled with sorrow and joy. This cavern was her cathedral, the pictures were gods of her own creation. This is where she had been when her family group disappeared. This was all that was left of her world.

Her eyes glazed over with tears, and for the first time since they had met, she smiled.

Chapter 9

Angel slept fitfully. The hunger and thirst that gnawed at her guts was fading. The fears that wormed through her mind like poisonous serpents had fled. She dreamed she was running through a sunlit meadow. Something was wrong! The sunlight shattered, the meadow turned into desert. She had never run in her life.

She woke with a start. There was nothing to see, nothing to hear but the sounds of her own breathing, and of blood pounding through her veins. She yawned in confusion, reached forward in the darkness, and touched a small boulder. It moved.

The Jewel in the Cave

She worked it free and drew it closer, squirmed onto her side and passed it down to her other hand which reached up as far as her breast. After jiggling the rock down to her knees, she rolled this way and that until it disappeared behind her.

She was desperate for water again. There had once been a small pool in the cavern behind her, but it had dried to dust thousands of years ago. She had brought no water with her. A bottle or a packet of food might have prevented her from squeezing through the narrowest parts of the tunnel.

She wondered if she had been gone longer than she thought. She had wakened from her sleep in the cavern, thinking ninety minutes had passed. But what if twelve hours and ninety minutes had passed? Her smartphone would read nearly the same. It would have said a.m. or p.m., but she hadn't noticed. She didn't enter the low narrow tunnel until the end of their first week underground. Daytime and night had become irrelevant.

What if she had slept through an entire day? That would account for her terrible thirst. It might account for why there was no one on the end of her safety line. They had given up on her; perhaps they had gone to the surface for help.

She reached forward and grasped another small piece of stone, this time an irregular shape, not a boulder. She worked it along her body, then shimmied back and forth until she could tell by the absence of pressure that it was behind her.

Without daring to dream this could be an escape from oblivion, she continued to move pieces of stone until, with a shock, she realized there was no more room at her feet. When she pushed back, the debris behind her was solid. With rock behind her and rock in front, she had dug herself into a grave.

She dropped her head. The side of her face rested against rubble and silt. She was too exhausted to cry.

THE JEWEL IN THE CAVE

CHAPTER 10

MEme and the boy settled into the outer cavern for a few days to restore their energy before travelling north A couple of dogs returned to the entrance, but didn't come in. MEme wanted them to go away, to forage for their own food, to return to the wild. She and her friend hunted a little, just enough to get by. And she spent hours in the sunlight, exposed to the insects, looking out over the landscape to where the great forest showed as a dark band on the horizon.

In the past, she and her people had ventured no more than a half-day's journey into the forest, and they always returned to open landscape by nightfall. There were fearsome people who lived there. She had never seen them, but she knew how they looked. The elders in her group had drawn pictures in the sand, and made signs with their hands, pressing their noses flat, pulling in their chins, walking with their arms drooping at their sides. Stocky people, stooped at the shoulders, with large heads and sloping brows, they seldom came out of the forest.

But she was certain it was them; they had taken her family.

For food? She knew humans did such things, especially the strangers with sloping foreheads. They would keep her family alive and penned up. They would eat them, one at a time.

Unless she rescued them; unless they escaped.

One of them had, a long time ago. A woman of their group had wandered off into the north and disappeared. The vanished woman was discovered by a foraging party at the edge of the forest. She was wrapped warmly in thick furs and appeared well fed, but before they cleaned up the blood leaking from her body, she died. They took the furs for themselves and scattered a thin layer of earth over her remains.

As they were preparing to leave someone noticed the burial mound twitching. They scooped back the earth, cut open the dead woman with a serrated clam shell, and pulled out a living baby girl. Then they buried the woman again.

Someone who had been nursing her own baby was among their number. Her baby had expired two days earlier, but she still had milk. She was given the newborn infant to suckle.

The story of being born out of the earth was MEme's own. It puzzled her and frightened her and gave her strength. It allowed her to see things others couldn't see, to connect opposing worlds others couldn't connect. She saw animals in rock and released them with paint. She understood how one thing could stand for another, how words could be made from the shape of a sound.

Looking about her, everything reminded her of all she had lost.

When the boy returned with a rabbit he'd caught in a snare made of animal sinew, she was still distressed. He sat down to comfort her and showed her a treasure he kept in his waist-band—the other half of her amber disc. He held it up. She held hers against it. They were a perfect match. His mother, or one of his mothers, the woman who first showed MEme the amber sphere that looked like the yolk of a small egg, had given it to the boy as he set out on his perilous journey to catch up with the girl. It was a form of blessing.

Early the next morning, MEme and her friend with no name—because he had not yet grasped sound-patterns as words—set out for the north.

The wind and the rain had covered the tracks of the marauders and their captives. Now, however, she knew where they had gone, and she followed their route with unerring precision. She read the landscape by day and the stars by night, the same way butterflies travel vast distances to find home, the same way birds fly thousands of miles to nest where they were born and whales swim half way around the planet to feed.

After walking a few hours, the boy demanded to know where they were going. She tried to evoke the fearsome people they were pursuing by hunching over, pressing her nose flat into her face, and grunting unintelligibly. She started to move forward without him. He sat on the ground and stared at his hands. She returned to his side and tried without words to explain further, in more detail.

Once he understood they were up against cannibals, he tried to dissuade her, first with gestures, then with restraint. She pushed him away.

He was bewildered, but when she moved on he followed and soon caught up. They walked side by side. Sometimes they exchanged sounds. The sounds had no precise meaning yet conveyed their fears and pleasures, their interests and things that annoyed them.

Several days later they passed beyond the horizon into the darkness of the forest, where MEme had been raised from her birth-mother's grave. She had many mothers — each woman in the tribe was a mother in her own way — but here she connected with the woman who had given her life.

The unfamiliar sounds and smells of the bush were troubling. They pressed on. When they came upon gnawed bones and chewed gristle strewn haphazardly, MEme and her friend knew they were closing in on the marauders.

They came to a deserted camp by a river. Footprints in the clay, left by narrow feet with high insteps, were all in a group. There were impressions of larger, broader feet meandering freely. These were from another human species, the fearsome humans who held her family clustered together as captives.

The river was deep and fast. It seemed

impassable. The boy indicated that perhaps these others had traveled upstream or downstream. But there was no sign of them leaving their campsite in either direction. They must have crossed.

Neither MEme nor the boy knew much about water. It was to drink or to wash away itches and sores.

They camped on the bank, and MEme gazed at the moving water for hours and then days. The boy watched her and waited for her to show she was ready to turn back. But she needed to know if any of her people were alive. She needed to know where they had been taken. And most of all, she needed to know if it was possible to rescue them.

One morning they awakened in a world of amber. Their camp was flooded by the light of the rising sun. While they were gnawing cold rabbit left from the night before, they were startled by a great slapping sound from the river. MEme had heard it before, but this time something clicked in her mind.

She got up and walked along the bank, curious but wary of man-eating reptiles. She had seen crude sketches of crocodiles drawn on the sand with human parts hanging out of their mouths. Rounding a bend, she looked out over the water and saw a giant beaver swimming leisurely upstream. She recognized the beaver from sketches by older hunters who had seen them. It was the size of a small auroch. Its teeth were large and blunt, it's eyes were slits, and its snout was rounded. It looked gentle, despite its size.

Maneuvering with its feet and its huge flat tail, the beaver pushed and pulled a fallen tree away from the shore, then began swimming with a branch of the tree clutched in its mouth. Sometimes it would release its grip and push the log with its head. As the log swept by, MEme saw how it had been moved into the center of the river. By the time it passed from sight, it was almost on the far bank.

She called the boy to join her and they followed downstream and, sure enough, the tree was being hauled and pushed into position in a pile of wood, small boulders, and mud on the other side.

MEme was thrilled. She led her friend back to their camp, then upstream to the beaver's cache of felled trees.

By now the boy understood. Without any exchange of directions, they pushed a log out into the current. Clinging to branches with their hands, they let the river sweep them downstream. As the log edged into the center of the river, they kicked and pushed harder, and when they came to a sharp bend the current carried them onto the far shore.

MEme hauled the log close to the beaver lodge, while the boy watched in wonder. Beside the lodge were other logs bound together with tree roots and vines. Somehow the sloped-head people had used these logs to cross over the river with their captives.

The fearless young woman and her friend proceeded on their northward journey among the trees, full of fear and admiration. Their enemy was cruel, but very smart.

That night they made new spears and sharpened them in the fire, burning the tips and grinding them against rock. When they crossed the river, they had left their old spears and the cooked remains of the rabbit behind, taking with them only the skins wrapped around their waists. She fell asleep beside the fire, clutching her piece of amber tight in her hand. When she awoke in the morning the boy was gone.

The Jewel in the Cave

Chapter 11

Angel's low narrow grotto became gradually warmer from her body heat. Beads of sweat rolled down her forehead and burned her eyes. She blinked and squinted, then kept them closed since there was nothing to see. She was inside a limestone coffin. Sweat pooled between her shoulder blades, and she felt the silver medallion cool on her back. It was a reminder that she was alive. With its amber replacement, it was also a reminder that she was connected to the woman whose paintings adorned the cavern behind her.

The girl, the fearless young woman, thought

Angel—she is me. ME, me, we are memes of each other. MEme was her name. She must have been buried in the cave; the amber disc was a burial charm. Her body had turned to dust but the jewel remained. And all these centuries later, it was still cool and warm, liquid to the eye but as hard as glass to the touch.

The medallion slid sideways on Angel's back. She wriggled to stifle an itch. A shoulder cramped. She stretched an arm into the empty darkness to relieve the pain. Her fingers touched rock. Instinctively, she grasped it and pulled the rock to her. When it banged against her helmet she removed the helmet and ran her fingers through her tangled hair. A wisp of cool air played softly against her forehead. She stiffened and stayed very still.

A cool thread laced tiny circles on her skin. Cool air! She breathed deeply and drew it into her lungs.

Cool fresh air.

Her mind reeled. Escape was possible.

She returned to her labors. Every rock

she pushed past her into the darkness behind brought her closer to the end. She forgot about hunger and thirst and exhaustion. She slowed from a frantic pace to a methodical routine, pushing out one stone, one piece of rock, one at a time.

She knew the myth of Sisyphus. He was condemned by the ancient Greek gods to push a huge boulder up a steep hill. When he reached the top, the boulder would roll back down and he'd have to start over again. Endlessly.

Sometimes that's how life felt. Endlessly overwhelming. But then Angel would smash the boulder she was pushing, whatever it was, into pieces. She would carry the pieces up the hill and pile them in a structure so they couldn't move. Sometimes the structure was a house, where she invited the gods for tea. They never came; perhaps they were ashamed she had outwitted them. Perhaps she was too proud to deserve their company. She tried never to be proud nor to shame others, not even the gods, but she was determined, always, not to let a boulder, a disability, despair, keep her down.

Now, here she was, moving stones past her body like the labors of Sisyphus. And she would keep doing so until she was dead. She inched her way forward; it seemed like forever. Then, she heard water trickling over rock. It was the first sound that was not from her own body scraping against tunnel walls or churning inside. The sounds gave shape to the darkness as the air opened around her.

She squirmed forward, then raised her head. Her helmet didn't clang against rock. She reached out to the sides. Nothing. She was in the cavern where they had set up their camp in a flat area beside a small stream.

She called. There was no one to answer.

"I'm alive," she shouted. Her voice echoed through the empty cavern, shouting back at her with her own useless words.

"I'm alone," she muttered so quietly even the limestone didn't respond.

The Jewel in the Cave

Chapter 12

The fearless young woman walked in slow circles around the cold fire pit, each circle a little wider than the one before. As she walked, she scanned the horizon, looking for her friend. Finally, she gave up and returned to the pit.

His spear was missing.

She began walking in circles again, this time looking downwards. Not far away, she saw the huge footprints of a saber-toothed cat. They seemed to crisscross over her friend's. One was following the other. It was impossible to say which was the hunter and which the hunted.

She followed the tracks, looking for blood.

When the tracks of the boy and the cat disappeared into rocky terrain, she turned and followed her own tracks back to the campsite. She sat by the fire pit and stared into the charred embers. She remained sitting like that for the entire day. As evening approached she got up for a drink from a small stream, then returned with a bundle of sticks and lit a fire. She gathered more wood and heaped it on the fire so that the flames licked high in the sky and could be seen from miles away.

She heard animals through the night, some real, some imagined. She heard howling, crying, a rabbit screaming in the jaws of a wildcat, a snake slithering through grass. At dawn, she decided she had to move on.

After walking half a day, she heard thumping of feet on the turf behind her. She turned with her spear raised. The sounds of footfalls betrayed no hesitation. Even before he came into sight she knew it must be her friend. Only a human would approach so directly, with neither fear nor guile.

The Jewel in the Cave

The boy was carrying a bloodied bundle which he dumped at her feet. He grinned with pride. He was presenting her with the severed head of a saber-toothed cat. It was the size of his own head, with two great teeth protruding down from its upper jaw. Although it's eyes were glazed with a thin milky film as they dried out from the heat, it looked remarkably ferocious. Its neck trailed sinews and blood. The missing body made it somehow more sinister, as if it had passed only part way through from another world, a spirit world, where it still lived. She could see it as a whole animal, magnificent in its power and grace, but she could not avoid looking at the ghastly remains of a dead thing, a pathetic trophy lying before her.

Since the heat of the sun was keeping them warm and they needed to travel lightly, he had not bothered with the skin.

He chattered unintelligible sounds.

She placed a hand on his arm, then turned away and continued her journey.

He picked up his trophy and followed. At

some point over the next few hours he let the cat's head slip from his hands, and it rolled into a patch of open sunlight where ants immediately began to devour it, starting with the viscera hanging from the neck and the hardening gel of the eyeballs.

THE JEWEL IN THE CAVE

CHAPTER 13

Oddly, the open space of the cavern seemed more oppressive to Angel than the low narrow burrow she had left behind. Dismissing panic as impractical, she squirmed toward the gurgling stream and dropped her face into the ice-cold water, gulping mouthful after mouthful until she had to come up for air. Satisfied, she moved across the sandy-clay floor worn smooth by her friends' feet and found herself clambering over gear they'd left behind. Here and there she encountered mounds of discarded clothing and ridges of fine dust. She found a backpack lying on its side, and rummaged through it until her fingers tangled in the soft wool of an alpaca sweater. From that, she knew the pack belonged to their team leader, David Slocombe. The connection was reassuring. She found a spare flashlight at the bottom of the pack, surrounded by laundry, a tangle of underwear and socks. When she switched on the light, suddenly the surrounding subterranean world loomed into view. It seemed oppressive and overwhelming at first; a huge chamber with a swooping ceiling and irregular walls.

The heaps of clothing scattered around, each a complete outfit, seemed odd. Dr. Slocombe normally insisted they keep the camp neat. What distracted her from poor housekeeping, however, was something not there. Where were the bats? She scanned the ceiling of the cave with her flashlight. Normally there would be thousands of bats, but now there were none.

Perhaps it was nighttime in the world outside. The bats had left to hunt insects and vermin in the dark. They would return in a rush at the break of day.

The Jewel in the Cave

Scanning the walls, she could make out the figures of animals painted among the shadows and planes of rock. They did not spring to life. There was nothing magical about them. Some showed the contours of flexed muscles. These, she believed, were painted by men. Others were mythic, putting antlers on lions, a terrifying smile on the faces of cats. These were by women. Women knew the secret lives of the animals they painted; men knew their movements. But none in this outer cave made the rocks breathe, tremble, or shriek in triumph or terror.

Angel surveyed the scene. Other backpacks, including her own, leaned against rock ledges near sleeping mats. Sleeping bags were neatly rolled on top of the mats, in spite of the clothing littered about. A camp stove and a box of plates, cups, and cutlery dominated a raised area which had served as their kitchen. Off to one side, a path worn into the silt led to a small chemical toilet behind a cluster of boulders. Over it, a wooden bar dangled in the air from a rope fixed overhead. This was for Angel, so she could hoist herself up when needed. As it was at the moment.

Returning to the shadows near her own sleeping mat, she saw a leather harness lying uselessly on the ground — it was a system of straps she had designed so that two strong people could carry her on a seat slung between them. She had hired local Frenchmen to carry her in. They would return when summoned by smartphone. She searched all the packs; no working phones. Perhaps the others had already called from the exit at the surface when they left.

No; she knew that was wishful thinking. She would have to proceed on her own.

She scooped fresh clean water from the stream until her thirst was quenched, then filled an empty thermos to carry with her. There were packets of dried food in a grub-box in the kitchen area, but no fuel for the stove. Two different backpacks yielded four and a half energy bars. She turned off her flashlight to conserve power, and settled back to eat and drink in the absolute dark. She tried to "slow-cook" some powdered stew by holding it in her mouth with a mouthful of water. It tasted like slime and grit. She spit it out and ate the half energy bar, which was mostly a wad of sickeningly sweet chocolate and very old peanuts.

The darkness was comforting, shielding her from the looming shadows and the absence of her colleagues. Whatever had happened, she knew they weren't coming back. She would have to wriggle and squirm on her belly to reach open air on her own.

In preparation, she crawled into her sleeping bag for a few hours of much needed sleep.

Chapter 14

Taking their bearings from sunlight breaking through overhead branches and from the moss growing away from the sun on the north sides of boulders and trees, MEme and her friend proceeded in a northerly direction until the ground fell abruptly away. A deep valley appeared where a river at the bottom had carved through the earth over millions of years. They gazed at terrain that seemed familiar but strange.

This was where humans like herself might live; or the other kind, the heavy-set humans with flat faces and no foreheads or chins.

The Jewel in the Cave

MEme touched her small nose, then grasped her chin as if testing to see that it was well-set and strong. She pushed her hair back from her face and set out with her friend to make their way along the top of the valley, often looking down, hoping to catch a glimpse of their fearsome adversary.

They knew they were getting close when the odors of humans drifted past them. Gradually, the noises of a thriving community stirred the air. She could not tell what her companion felt, whether it was fear or excitement, but she felt shivers of anticipation. The look on his face suggested he was prepared to prove himself in a fight to the death. She realized death would be foolish if it could be avoided.

They edged into the dark folds of some bushes to look down on the encampment. She was surprised at how many of these strange creatures there were. An attack would be suicide. But before they did anything she needed to confirm that at least some of her family was alive. If they were already dead and consumed, there was no point in continuing. She and the boy would return home. They would start a family of their own.

She crept forward to get a better view into the shadows below. She heard familiar sounds of distress. The boy pulled her back, then crept forward himself. She held onto his legs to keep him from sliding over the edge. He went further and then twisted his body to glance at her over his shoulder. His eyes were round and his nostrils flared. They were there! He must have seen them huddled against the rocky slope.

His legs were sweaty. Suddenly he was sliding. Her fingernails cut into his flesh. She couldn't hold him. He tumbled and careened through the air, crashing against dead branches of dwarf trees that were clinging to the slope.

He shrieked in pain as he disappeared. There was a moment of stunned silence. Then the human-like creatures raised a huge noise of calling and chattering, fearful at first and then menacing, as they closed around the boy who'd fallen from the sky.

The Jewel in the Cave

The air filled with a piercing scream. At first MEme thought her friend had been murdered. But the way the scream rose in pitch and trailed off slowly, she knew it was a message for her. Letting her know he was alive, warning her to hide, telling her that her family was safe. For the time being.

Even as she ran upstream, parallel to the river, she thought about how clearly she understood what he meant. She could see his message without words in her head.

Where the land sloped more gently to the river she stopped to catch her breath. She knew they would come searching for her. They were hunters; they would find evidence she had been where the boy had fallen.

Hauling a driftwood stump free from the shore, she waded into the river. Rivers no longer scared her. Water was no longer threatening.

She kicked away from the shallows and kept low among the twisted roots of the floating stump. By the time it drifted into sight of the encampment, she was comfortably out from the shore. Even if they saw her, she was beyond the range of their spears.

Then her stump became caught in an eddy in the river's flow. Rocky outcroppings created a whirlpool, sending the water swirling against the main current. Her refuge began drifting towards shore near a cluster of the flat-nosed humans.

Holding onto roots hidden under the water, she kept as low as she could. When it seemed her stump would carry her immediately in front of the people, she took a deep breath and slipped under the surface without leaving a ripple.

She gazed upwards on an angle. She could see their distorted faces. The way the water bent light, they looked like monstrous beasts.

The stump stopped moving. She became desperate for air. Her lungs ached; she was choking, she was going to throw up, her hands were shaking, the world shimmered with blackness.

She slowly raised her head into the air and

gasped.

The monsters were children, mostly girls. They were washing, playing in the shallows. They were fascinated by the floating tree stump. When it appeared to have a head, with hazel eyes and reddish-brown hair like their own, and a gasping mouth, they fell utterly silent.

MEme expected them to scream.

They stood perfectly still.

She smiled. They smiled.

MEme felt with her feet until she found a solid rock to push against. She thrust her weight downwards, forcing her stump free of the shore. The eddying water swung it into the whirlpool, then released it back into the current.

Still caught up in its roots, she raised herself as high as she could out of the water. She waved at the chinless children with flat noses and sloped foreheads. They waved back, smiling, accepting a kinship they shared. She smiled in return, then disappeared under the water and came up hidden in shadows.

The stump floated away.

A boy of another species had fallen from the sky. A girl had appeared from the depths of the river and then disappeared. The world was only a little stranger than these children already suspected. They went back to playing and splashing in the shallows.

Behind them, a sumptuous dinner was being prepared. The fires were already blazing. When the flames died down, huge quantities of fresh meat would be slaughtered and roasted over the sizzling coals.

THE JEWEL IN THE CAVE

CHAPTER 15

Angel awakened in the absolute dark. She lay on top of her sleeping bag, staring at nothing. How do blind people know they exist, she wondered? By touch, by sound, by other senses kicking in? Of course. She was appalled by her own stupidity. She had never thought much about disabilities other than her own. You deal with whatever you're dealt. So long as you're conscious, everything else is a bonus. She thought of herself as "differently abled." But *abled*, she was. And *different*, for which she was thankful.

Otherwise, how would she have ended up

the last person in the world, a mile from the surface of the earth?

She switched on her flashlight and surveyed her surroundings. What an odd place to be, with her only companion the ghost of a young woman who had turned rock into something alive, fifty thousand years before Angel was born..

She switched off her flashlight.

Would a search party come looking for her? Why had her companions gone off in a rush, leaving their equipment behind? Why would they force her to fend for herself? When the safety line got snagged, did they think a cave-in had killed her? When the line disappeared, did they think it was a signal she could never get out? Did they flee their own terrors? Her mind swarmed with possibilities. None were reassuring.

Questions with no answers. At least, not for now. She realized if she were going to survive, she would have to make plans.

She turned on her flashlight and gathered

The Jewel in the Cave

the thermos of water, the remaining energy bars, and a few packets of dried pea soup. She stuffed them into her sleeping bag, along with a change of underwear, a sweater, and a rain proof jacket from her backpack. She changed her mind and took the jacket out to wrap around her notebook. She found several other notebooks in the scattered gear. She was surprised they had been left behind, but added them to her waterproof bundle. Hauling herself through littered clothing and ridges of grey powder, she placed the bundle on a flat rock at the center of the camp. Whatever happened to her, to the others, someone, someday, would discover their records of discovery.

She had written nothing of the breathtaking animals in the innermost cavern. MEme's paintings were much too personal, too magical, too special, to describe in mere words. Someday, perhaps, she would present them to the world. If she died before reaching the surface, it gave her comfort to know these jewels in a cave were buried under the same limestone that would be her own grave.

After determining exactly which direction to go, she tied her sleeping bag with a short line around her ankles so she could drag it along, then she extinguished the flashlight. She would need it again wherever the tunnels diverged or the caverns became a confusion of rock-slides and false passages. She had a long way to go.

"Okay then," she said to her echo, which whispered back in return.

With the fearless young woman and her secrets behind her and the promise of daylight ahead, she plunged into the darkness.

THE JEWEL IN THE CAVE

CHAPTER 16

MEme crept through the underbrush near the edge of the river. As she got closer to the encampment, she tried not to think about the sweet smell of cooking meat wafting in the air. The valley was in deep shadow by the time she got close enough to see people gathered around the fire. They were cooking chunks of meat on long sticks. Flames sometimes flared when fat dripped into the coals. In the flickering light, they could have been her own species of human. The very fact that the meat being prepared smelled so good made her sick.

By the time these others started tearing

off morsels with their teeth, the sun had been swallowed in darkness. She could hear their lips smacking and see their faces glisten with grease in the firelight.

She moved forward, keeping as low as she could. Suddenly a wavering shadow crossed her path. A man was standing between her and the fire. She cringed into the shadows. Did he see her? He was looking her way. Then he turned to the side and peed into the bushes. She was so close she could hear the rattle of water on branches.

When he turned back to the fire, he would see her. She reached for the fragment of amber tucked into her leather bandeau. She slowly rose to her feet and crept forward. He was concentrating on what he was doing. When he was within reach, she yanked his head backward, exposing his neck. With her other hand she pressed the amber slice to his throat and started to rip into the flesh.

The man, who was shorter than her but much heavier, stayed perfectly still, as if resigned to his fate. His head tilted so that his eyes looked up into hers. Her hand stopped cutting. With her amber still in the open wound, she lowered him against her and the two of them sank to the ground. She twisted around to see his face gleaming in the firelight. His features were distorted from pain. He looked like people she knew. Especially his eyes. They were human like hers. They were hazel like hers. Not brown, like everyone else in her family. He had a scruffy red beard and auburn hair.

She held the amber twisted in the wound in his neck, then suddenly she jerked it away. He grasped his throat with his hands as blood seeped between his fingers. He shook from the pain, but he made no attempt to get away. If he struggled, they would be seen. His family would kill her. One of them had to die or they both would.

They gazed into each others' eyes. She glanced in the direction where her family was being held captive. He glanced at his family by the fire, who were happily unaware of the drama playing out beside them.

Their eyes locked. She recognized something of herself in this man. Perhaps he saw something of himself in her. She felt her grip loosening. Was it because he was human, a different species but much like herself? Did the kinship between them run deeper? Deep enough to prevent her from murdering him in cold blood?

As if understanding her dilemma, her captive took charge. He slowly reached for her hand with the amber piece in her fingers. He took a firm grip and raised her hand, setting the amber into the open wound in his throat. He winced from the pain, then without taking his eyes from hers, he ripped the amber deep into his flesh and drew it across to sever his windpipe.

His eyes flared wide as he died.

MEme had to shake herself free from conflicting emotions. She lowered the man's head to rest gently on the earth and slipped back into the darkness away from the fire. She followed close to the steep hillside, which soon became an overhanging cliff, passing shelters made from auroch skins stretched over poles leaning against the rock.

On the far side of the shelters, she saw a high fence made of sticks and small logs jammed into the ground. She knew her own people were penned behind the barricade. She edged closer to the pen, but stopped suddenly when she saw three men of the other species sitting with spears close by on the ground. She was puzzled. Their spears seemed to have pieces of stone attached to the ends. The sharpness of the tips was terrifying, even in the dark.

When someone behind the fence shuffled too close in her direction, perhaps catching her scent, one of the guards grabbed his spear and thrust it through an opening, forcing him back. Not before MEme recognized it was the boy. He must have seen her, because he was soon stirring her family to make distracting noises by chattering and wailing as if the world had come to an end.

She slipped through darkness to get closer to the rock wall, where she gathered some dry grasses and sticks. She made a bundle and slid it against a support pole at the base of a shelter. She unwrapped her leather bandeau and removed the fire-making stones, being careful to keep her chip of amber secure.

Bending over to shield what she was doing from the guards, who were distracted by the noise inside the barricade, she struck the flint to the iron pyrite. A fire immediately flared up. She skittered into the darkness as the shelter burst into flames.

The guards came running. Everyone in the village came running.

She hunched over and slipped past them, going the other way, and when she got to the fence she hauled open a heavy gate.

She made a gesture of plugging her ears, signaling silence. Quietly, her family slipped past her into the shadows upriver. The last to leave was her friend.

When he reached her, he took her in his arms

and shuddered, and whispered sounds that meant nothing, sounds that meant everything.

In the light of the fire growing behind them, she could see the deep scratches she had made on his legs, trying to stop him from falling. There were other scratches and bruises as well. He hobbled but moved on his own. Hand in hand, they followed the others into the flickering night.

By the long shadows they cast, she knew before long the entire settlement behind was ablaze. Still, when they reached a height of land and looked back, she was amazed to see soaring flames lick the stars. For a moment she felt pity, but that was displaced by continuing concern for her struggling family, many of whom followed along in bewilderment, not able to grasp that they had been rescued. The forest ahead seemed to swallow them into its darkness as firelight glinting on the trees was obscured the deeper they entered among them. When the shouts of the frantic marauders faded to silence, MEme knew it was safe to slow down.

As their little group trudged through the night, she thought of the man who had died in her arms. He had been a human like her, only different. He had embraced his own death. He could have fought her, she would have killed him, they both would have died. What had he been thinking? What had he been feeling? Why had he saved her? Did he recognize something in her of himself? As she had, of him, in her?

When the sun was emerging from the horizon to the east, they stopped by a stream to rest.

Her friend had been carrying a small boy and she, a small girl. They set the children down and wrapped their arms around each other. This time, they had nothing to say. They just rocked in each other's arms until their breath and their heartbeats were exactly the same. Then, shyly, they broke away and turned to help whoever needed their aid.

Many were wounded from the thrusts of stone tipped spears. Many were bruised from beatings. Many needed cuts and scrapes cleaned with damp moss from beside the stream.

As she nursed her people, she felt more comfortable about having ravaged their enemy, leaving their village in flames. Still, that moment of cruelty and sadness she and the dying man had shared continued to haunt her, as she knew it would for the rest of her life.

MEme looked around at her family. Despite their wounds and injuries, no one was missing. She was puzzled. She made motions to the boy to indicate eating. He shook his head. There was no food. They had not eaten in several days.

No, no. Who did the flat-nosed people eat at their feast? What was the sweet scent of meat she smelled in the air?

He pawed at the earth and growled and bared his teeth.

Wolf, they had eaten wolf.

She howled like a wolf and bared her teeth.

He shook his head, no. Not wolf. He waggled his bottom and let his tongue hang out. Dog.

Amidst the laughter at his canine impression,

MEme cried out in pain. Dogs were creatures who would die for their human partners. Her people did not eat dogs.

Attention shifted as two hunters from their group appeared. They had fashioned spears from sticks and had brought down an ibex. It still had horns and a beard. They carved the ibex into chunks. Some ate the bloodied meat raw. Others waited until MEme started a fire and cooked their pieces on sticks.

She sank down against a tree, exhausted.

The boy brought her a sizzling chunk of cooked meat and tore off small pieces for her with his teeth. Only when she was finished eating did he eat, himself. The others noticed.

A stranger who had fallen from the sky and was fierce and had frightened their captors, a boy who was gentle enough to feed his partner before himself, although he was not like themselves, was a man to admire.

She saw how they were thinking and smiled.

The Jewel in the Cave

CHAPTER 17

Angel found it more difficult to haul herself forward when there weren't the enclosing walls of a tunnel to grasp. To reach the surface was a long uphill climb; not so steep that they needed ropes and pulleys when they went in, but enough to make her progress getting out an exhausting challenge. Whenever she needed a rest, or was unsure of her direction, she turned on the flashlight and surveyed the scene. It was easy to follow footprints in the sandy clay, which all seemed to be going deeper into the cave she was trying to escape — except for two sets made by the work boots of the men who had carried her in. She and her colleagues wore expensive boots made of waterproof synthetics. The Frenchmen wore boots with steel toes made of rubber and leather.

It must be daylight outside by now, she imagined, yet no bats swooped past on their way to perch in the innermost caverns. This made her sad. She had seen no living thing for days, not even a spider or beetle, not even a bat.

She carried on, stopping a few times to gnaw on an energy bar. Eventually, fatigue overwhelmed her and she found a soft patch to spread out her sleeping bag. The atmosphere had become a little warmer, less damp. She rolled onto her bag and almost immediately fell into a dreamless asleep.

Suddenly, she was awakened by a whisper of fresh air on her cheek. With her flashlight still off, she surveyed the darkness ahead, looking for an opening, a sliver of light. All she saw were shadows and rock.

She ate the last of her energy bars and crept forward, breathing the fresh cool air, seeing nothing. Finally she was forced to stop. Her arms and shoulders refused to take her further. She dropped her head into the dirt and squinted her eyes, then opened them. The surrounding darkness had a tinge of color. She rolled onto her side and looked up. The blue-black sky of a moonless night was filled with stars overhead.

My God, she said to herself. She had expected daylight. It never occurred to her she would emerge in the night. My God, she repeated, as her eyes adjusted and she looked out over the rugged valley landscape across and below.

She drank the last of her water and, spreading the sleeping bag again, she crawled in and drew its warmth around her. She was too tired to do up the zipper.

Chapter 18

As they broke out of the forest and plodded toward home, MEme played with sounds in her head. Sometimes she said them aloud. Each time she did, the child on her back responded by nuzzling against her neck, leaning away and giggling, cooing, clicking her tongue, imitating the sounds.

MEme sensed she was on the verge of something important. Humans, like birds with their songs, like wolves with their howling, conveyed meaning by pitch and by tension — how high or low the sounds were, how smoothly or roughly they followed each other.

A high harsh squeal was terror, a low rumble was threatening, melody conveyed concern, a hum was contentment, short sharp noises demanded attention. They had songs without lyrics.

But what if *patterns* of sound could be shaped to convey the same meaning, over and over? In her cave drawings, lines and shading and colors made animals. They were not actual animals, and yet in her mind they were. What if sound could work the same way? Her mind soared with the possibilities. Everything could have a sound of its own.

She spoke her own pattern into the air, "MEme, MEme. MEme."

She set the child down when they stopped to rest. The little girl clutched her hand, looked up, and declared, "MEme. MEme. MEme."

This excited Meme, and she gazed around to find her young man. He was squatting by a pool, scooping water onto his face. "Plash," she said, trying to imitate the sound of the water.

The tiny girl holding her hand said

"Plash," then ran over and climbed onto the young man's back, nearly knocking him into the water. "Plash, Plash, Plash," she declared triumphantly. Then she clambered down and returned to MEme. Standing in front of her, she solemnly declared, "Gleau." And so her name became Gleau.

They decided to call the little boy Ginge. He was pleased, but he never used the name himself.

MEme and Gleau understood what they were doing with sounds. It was meaningless to the others. Humans had the capacity to make words, but the concept escaped them. They continued to chatter like birds and bullfrogs and wolves and ground squirrels. In order to understand that a pattern of sound could have meaning, they needed words. To create words, they had to understand that patterns of sound could have meaning.

Plash seemed mystified by the secrets MEme and her little friend shared. If he understood words at all, he found them a useless distraction.

He followed his half-formed thoughts as best he could, and urged the others to start moving again. Their enemy might have sent warriors out to punish them, to murder them all for causing the terrible fire.

And MEme feared retribution for the death of the man she had held in her arms.

None of her family knew he had died, that she had killed him, that he killed himself.

She wondered if her birth mother had spent the seasons of her disappearance with his people. Could a man like him be her father? This question, she believed, would haunt her for the rest of her life, even if she had not the words to express it.

They were three long days from home when they reached the big river. The water level had dropped and MEme insisted they wade across before nightfall. Something didn't feel right; the atmosphere was oppressive. She wanted to be on their own side before setting up camp.

No one had trouble accepting her as their leader. She was strong, she was smart, she was ferociously brave. Even Plash willingly followed her lead, although he was not from their group. Not everyone of their species mated for life, but he would be staying with her until one of them died.

As they settled in, a wall of darkness rose up from the west. Where usually the sun glowed crimson long after it sank into the earth, there was only an ominous black band that grew higher as the evening progressed. No one but MEme seemed to notice.

Later, by the fire, Plash tried to explain that the stocky marauders had been feasting on dog because her family was being kept alive until winter. It was easier to keep humans than dogs because humans helped to look after themselves. When it was cold enough to freeze their meat, they would have been slaughtered to provide food for the village through the hardest months. Anything left over in the spring would be thrown to the dogs.

All this, Plash managed to explain without words. He used hand gestures, facial expressions, a wide range of sounds.

Cannibalism was a strategy the flat-faced people had developed to combat the increasing cold and the scarcity of food. They did not eat their own kind. MEme's species was a favorite but they were difficult to catch, since every few generations they moved to escape the ice-age cold creeping down from the north. In spite of stone-tipped spears, these people were not so adept at dealing with the great sheet of ice moving south.

MEme snuggled in against Plash as the fire died down. They would get a good start in the morning.

Toward dawn, the whole family group awoke feeling restless. An eerie calm had fallen over the world. The night held its breath. A low rumble filled the air, the earth trembled, the stars disappeared.

A shrieking wind pierced the stillness. The river bed surged into a tumultuous flood. People scrambled to higher ground, wide-eyed, mouths twisted in fear. Woolly mammoths in the distance trumpeted their terror. Wolves howled piteously, dogs yipped in distress. Swarms of birds wheeled this way and that, screeching their fear.

Humans whimpered and screamed in despair.

The world was a living thing. Universal death was upon them.

Gleau and Ginge found MEme and the young man in the roiling darkness and crawled close against them, and cried. Birth parents had no special relationships with children. Even the mothers who bore them were simply one of the mothers who raised them. Special bonds sometimes formed that were more sacred than blood.

The roar and rumble continued as a thousand thunderstorms gathered beyond the horizon. Confused flashes of sheet lightning lit up the sky. With morning, these turned to forked lightning as the black sky cracked open again and again with slivers of deadly radiance. But no sun appeared. The people knew where to look, but the flashing dark sky hid the sun from their sight. All day long, as they followed its ghostly progress up and over and down in the west, the people stayed huddled together.

MEme had enough sense of the vastness of creation to realize the forest people would be victims of the same natural horrors. It was the world itself that was threatening to shatter.

The next day the sky was even darker, the green-grey color of putrid flesh. Even over the crackling of lightning and thunder, the wailing of the people filled the air.

Early on the third morning, although the sun had not risen again, MEme roused her young man. Each picked up a child who had taken them on as parents, and they began to walk.

The wailing stopped. Everyone watched as the small party of four trudged south through bleakness toward home. Then one by one, two by two, in small groups, the others gathered together and followed.

It was a long trek across open plains and

dried marshland. Some people dropped along the way. If they could be helped, they were. If not, they were left to die.

Eventually, the light changed from murky grey to purplish blue, indicating night was almost upon them. Absolute darkness rose all around.

The next day and the next were much the same. MEme followed her instincts, leading the way. They finally passed a rocky outcropping and climbed a gorge onto a plateau with a stream running through it. The water looked brackish, but they were back at their deserted village.

Everyone crowded inside the main cave. They lit a great fire from the firewood stacked against a back wall. By the light of the flames, each looked around to see who was missing. They had lost almost one third of their number. They settled into different nooks and spaces and gathered rushes scattered on the floor into beds.

At the break of dawn, several hunters went

out into the murky light. Plash, the young outsider, was among them. Almost immediately they came back in. Each was covered in a layer of thick dust. They shook dirt from their hair and coughed it out of their lungs.

MEme went to the entrance and looked out. It was raining soot.

She smiled to herself. They could deal with hunger for a few more days. If they were still out in the open they would have suffocated; they would all be dead.

Chapter 19

When Angel woke up it seemed like a day had passed and it was night time again. She was still so exhausted it hurt to move. She boosted herself to a sitting position and leaned against a rock wall by the side of the cave. Looking out through the gloom, she could make out roofs and the highway below. There were no lights, not from passing cars nor from homes. The gloom seemed unnatural, like a greenish-brown haze. There were no signs of life.

She was a scientist. She needed to figure this out. When she had gone to sleep, stars had filled the sky. It was like she could see forever. Now, high overhead, a wheel of light proclaimed it was actually the middle of the day. The sun was an amber disc, hovering in the murky sky.

The first thing she thought was that the problem must be herself. Perhaps her eyes had been damaged by debris in the tunnel or by the fine dust at the camp. But holding her hands in front of her, she could see every pore.

Then what else? There must be a volcano eruption close by, spewing clouds of ash into the air.

But there were no live volcanoes in the area.

A more dramatic explanation occurred to her.

Fifty thousand years ago, perhaps when MEme was alive, an asteroid made of iron struck the desert in Arizona. It left a crater nearly a mile wide and more than five hundred feet deep. The iron burnt up from the force of the crash, but clouds of ash blocked out the sun and spread in a thin layer that covered the world.

The hole in the Arizona landscape was

called the Beranger Crater. It was a popular tourist attraction.

Could there have been such a catastrophe? Surely, with all our modern equipment, astronomers would have seen the asteroid coming. Even if there was nothing to stop it, there would have been warnings.

Angel searched through her mind for another explanation. Nothing seemed more likely, no matter how unlikely an asteroid seemed.

She groped inside her clothes and, grasping the chain on her medallion, drew it into the muted light. The silver seemed dull, as if it would be soft to the touch. The amber absorbed light, so it reflected nothing, not even her own image. The sensation of not being there was eerie, like being in the darkness of a burrow, except now she could see her surroundings. She didn't believe in ghosts, but wondered if this was how a ghost might experience reality.

Defiantly she draped the medallion over her breast. Leaving her sleeping bag behind, she set out down the rocky hillside to the houses below. Sliding on her bottom, she was careful not to rip her coveralls or the flesh beneath them that had no feeling. As she approached the dark houses in the valley, an overwhelming shroud of foreboding settled over her. Something in the world was very wrong.

Chapter 20

It was the middle of the day and the world was dark. Black clouds hung in the air and ash fell in a fine dry rain. Everything was still. The eerie silence was penetrated only by the bleating of animals dying from hunger and choking with dirt in their mouths.

Behind MEme, people in the cave were desperate, some were moaning. They had no concept of the end of the world, but they understood death as the moment when everything stopped. Darkness had burnt up the sun and rained down from the sky. Most waited for their last breaths to be drawn. They waited for death to consume them.

Toward nightfall, the sun appeared like a fiery wheel on the horizon. Overhead, the sky was clear. MEme stepped out onto the ash that covered everything. It was not deep; it hardly rose up to cover her toes except when she walked. Then, it wrapped around her feet like dry water. She picked up a spear from beside the cave and carefully descended from their plateau onto the plain.

Some grasses were crushed to the ground, but some were standing in clumps. The winds had ripped bushes from the earth; some trees had been toppled. It was all very strange and unfamiliar.

By an upturned stump she found a whimpering auroch calf, lying close to its nearly dead mother. She pulled the calf away. The mother twisted her head but was too weak to lift it. She let out a deep sigh and died.

MEme searched around until she found a large chip of very hard stone. Using the stone as a knife, she cut through the auroch in front of its rear legs and stripped the skin back. With a slicing motion she cut off large chunks of sirloin. The meat was warm. She bundled the steak into a bag made of the auroch's skin and heaved it over her shoulder.

The calf's brown eyes followed her every movement during the butchering. As MEme walked away with her bundle, the calf seemed to sigh in despair and settled back into the dirt.

She stopped, went back to the calf, and hoisted it onto its feet. It wobbled. A wet umbilical cord dangled from its belly, but it did not seem to be injured. She gazed up the slope toward the camp, then briefly rubbed the calf between the ears, picked up her bundle, and began climbing.

Halfway up the steep slope, she stopped and turned to see the calf clambering awkwardly among the rocks, trying to stay with her. When the calf caught up, she waited a few minutes so it could rest, then together, they climbed the rest of the way to the plateau.

Plash came out of the cave with Gleau and

Ginge in tow. He took the bundle of meat from her, muttering sounds of wonder and thanks. He looked at the auroch calf that was leaning against MEme's legs. Her hand rested on its head.

MEme took back the meat and motioned for the young man to stay with the calf. The children followed her as she went inside the cave with her bundle and opened it on the floor in front of the fire.

People gathered. In the midst of misery, she had brought comfort. She motioned for them to help themselves and for one of her mothers to feed the children, then went back out. Plash was stroking the calf.

He had touched only dead animals before this, except for dogs that hung around camp and begged for scraps. And people—he had touched the flat-faced people who picked him up after he fell from the sky and beat him and threw him into the pen.

He seemed confused by the calf.

He was a hunter. He had killed aurochs.

Full-grown, an auroch cow could easily kill a human. But several humans with spears could kill an auroch. A pack of humans together could kill a mammoth. Even a very young hunter could kill an auroch calf.

He had killed a saber-toothed cat by himself.

He stroked the calf between the ears and let it nuzzle against him.

MEme knew the forest people kept animals, even humans, for future nourishment. Was this where she got the idea? She pushed her hair back from her high forehead.

Plash entered the cave and cut off a big piece of sirloin from the chunk of auroch meat. He roasted the meat on a stick over the flames and went back out and gave MEme an even half. They took shelter beneath an overhang of rock and brushed the layer of dirt from their bodies.

The calf chewed on a clump of grass and watched as they ate.

A woman who had lost her infant squeezed milk into a shallow gourd bowl for the calf to drink.

MEme spent the rest of the day building a corral between the stone wall by the cave and the stream that ran across their plateau. It was a shorter version of the fence in the squat people's camp where her family had been held captive. After Plash saw what she was doing, he helped. No one else did. They didn't seem to understand, not even when she guided the auroch calf into the pen and closed the gate, not even when she gathered a sheaf of grasses poking up through the sooty dirt and offered it to the calf as food.

Over the next few days, some of the younger men roamed the area and brought back meat of animals who were dying from hunger and thirst. It wasn't hunting so much as gathering. Sometimes they explained with hand gestures that an auroch cow had died shielding a calf. Because they assumed MEme must hold them sacred, they brought the living calves back and she put them in the pen.

Wind shifted the dirt into drifts. Grasses

grew up again. People moved into other caves along the cliffside. MEme and Plash and Gleau and Ginge were finally on their own.

What might have been the end of the world had left nothing more than a thin layer of ash spread across the face of the earth. And a fear in the humans that it might happen again.

When winter approached, they had a small herd of cattle. As the winters grew colder, as year by year the ice sheet crept down from the north, MEme's people would never starve. She knew this, although she did not have the words to explain it, not even to herself.

She named things and tried to teach the children these names. There was no turning back. Language was a new technology. It was here to stay. Some of the older people tried to avoid it. They feared words would get mixed up with the actual world. They feared they would lose what was real.

One day, while Gleau and Ginge were still small, MEme made a torch from dried branches and led them with Plash into the depths of the cave. The children had never been there before. Plash had, but only once. He knew what to expect. He was excited. The kids were excited.

Together, the family walked through silence, their feet soundlessly treading over the dust of eons. They could hear their own breathing; they could hear their heartbeats as if they were one.

They walked through narrow passages, crept through tunnels made by rivers when the earth was young, clambered through small caverns and cracks in the rock, until they reached a low and narrow passage, where they had to crawl on hands and knees. Eventually they entered MEme's secret chamber. The children screamed with fear and delight when the torchlight gleamed on animals that leaped from the stone. Aurochs and mammoths and saber-toothed cats, antelopes and bison, hippos and horses, raced over the walls at a dazzling speed. Their soft colors, their powerful lines, shimmered in the flickering torchlight.

MEme handed the torch to Plash, then

squatted beside a flat rock and set a cooked piece of auroch fat on top. Scooping up some ashes from the fire pit, she mixed them with the fat and used a smaller rock to grind the mixture into a dark paste. She squatted over the rock and peed a little. The children who had watched in wonder giggled. Adults usually peed in the shadows. She stirred the mixture into a black liquid.

Taking a straw from the dried grass on the floor, she scooped up some liquid. She held her free hand against the wall and blew the mixture from the tube. When she lowered her hand, there was its outline, her signature, on the wall.

She did the same for Plash, and then for Gleau and Ginge.

Four handprints to prove they had once been alive.

CHAPTER 21

Angel skittered rapidly across the highway. While sliding down the hillside she had not seen a single vehicle, but it wouldn't hurt to be wary. She could easily be run over in the twilight gloom by a driver who'd assume she was only a bump on the road. Except it wasn't twilight. The orange ball overhead was the sun, marking the time as mid-day.

A single light appeared as she approached houses on the side road running through the village. It was in the front room of a cottage at the edge of the clearing that appeared to be "off the grid." There were no electrical wires leading to it, and the south-facing roof was covered in solar panels. It seemed likely a power failure was responsible for the darkness everywhere else.

Swinging her weight onto one elbow, Angel reached as high as she could to knock on the door. She didn't want people inside to think the noise was an animal butting against the wood. As she waited, she listened. There were no sounds of animals at all. In a village this size, the air should be filled with small sounds. She expected to hear people gossiping, canes tapping, people working their gardens; cattle lowing, sheep and goats beeping, dogs barking, cats meowing, dooryard chickens clucking to be fed. Instead, she heard silence. It was as ominously oppressive as the silence she had endured deep in the earth.

She twisted the knob and pushed open the door. She callout out in a loud voice, "*Allo, allo, ce n'est que moi.*" Hello, hello, it is only me. "*C'est moi.*" It's me. "Angel." She paused. "*Pas un ange.*" Not an angel. "*Angelique,* Angelica

Harris."

The place was deserted, but it was good to hear her own voice in a human environment.

She switched on a couple more lights. After a few minutes a generator outside the back door kicked in. The lamp in the window had been running on batteries that needed to be charged once more lights were turned on. The generator would eventually run out of gas and fail.

The inside of the cottage was sparsely furnished. The main living area was dominated by a large television set against one wall. Across from it were a matching sofa and a plush easy chair that looked like they had been rescued from a charity store. The occupants were up-to-date with technology, but either cheap or determined to recycle old stuff. Sitting on a coffee table made of old boards and used bricks, an arrangement of wildflowers in an old pickle jar had begun to wilt. There was no evidence of children around, no toys on the floor, no family photos. There were a few books piled neatly beside the easy chair.

Drawing herself to the center of the room, Angel felt she knew the couple who lived here. Middle-aged, perhaps elderly, self-sufficient; one of them was a reader, but mostly they watched the world pass by on television, their window on a troubled world, a world they chose to avoid.

A pile of material on the floor beside the easy chair turned out to be a complete set of women's clothing. Socks, not stockings, protruded from worn slippers set close to an apron over a crumpled dress with flashes of underwear peeking through the folds. Angel hoisted herself onto the chair and looked over to see a complete men's outfit laid out on the sofa, as if the man wearing them had vanished and they had collapsed where he'd been. A column of grey dust rose from his collar to a larger patch in the indentation on a pillow where his head would have been. At the other end of the sofa, dust ran from the cuffs of his trousers into his socks. She looked down to examine the old woman's clothes more carefully. The same fine dust spread out, as if it had scattered when her garments fell to the floor.

She touched the grey dust with the tips of her fingers, then wiped them clean. This was the residue when organic materials were cremated. She had seen it in the lab; she had seen it in her mother's burial urn.

Horror crept over her as she tried to understand.

The last living things she had experienced were MEme's painted rock walls, and they were an illusion. She remembered dust ridges at the campsite. She had crawled through them as she pushed empty clothing aside. There were no bats in caverns that should have been swarming with bats. When she emerged from the depths of the earth, the world was still there, exactly as she left it, but all life had vanished, leaving only dust in its wake.

Chapter 22

The winter after the end of the world was hard. In the autumn, MEme and Plash stored dry grasses in their cave to feed auroch calves huddled against the stone wall by the stream. The calves grew fat. When it was time, when the humans were very hungry, MEme lifted a rock above the head of the first calf they had rescued. He was now a sleek young bull. She smashed the rock down, shattering the young bull's skull. She dropped the rock and held the bull's head as he slowly collapsed to the ground.

Then she walked away, leaving it to others

to cut up his body for meat.

In the late spring, when the hillsides were a riot of blue and purple flowers, MEme retired to her cave to give birth to twins. The first came quickly. She was small. When the second came out, he took a single deep breath and expired.

The women took the surviving infant from her. MEme was too weak to protest. The women carried the living twin girl onto the plateau and exposed her to sunshine. The baby closed her eyes against the light, clenching and unclenching her tiny fingers.

For one twin to survive was considered unlucky. For the survivor to be a girl was worse. MEme knew that's what her people believed. She refused to accept their beliefs. She struggled to her feet, and with Plash's support she followed them. Blood ran down her legs, and she was trembling as they approached her abandoned infant. The women backed away. She was the woman born out of the earth. They would not defy her. She reached down to pick up her baby, but faltered. Plash took the girl gently into his arms, and MEme leaned on him as they slowly climbed up into their cave. Gleau and Ginge joined them inside. The dead infant was nowhere in sight. The women had disposed of his body.

For the next week the children helped care for their mother, but MEme weakened. Plash found a woman who had recently lost her own baby. He brought her to be a wet-nurse, feeding her own milk to the infant because MEme couldn't manage.

MEme died quietly. Plash prepared a torch of dried sticks, which he bound carefully into a bundle. He lit the torch from the fire and handed it to Gleau. He lifted MEme's body into his arms. Leaving the baby with the wet-nurse, and with Gleau and Ginge leading the way with the torch, they set out on a journey deep into the earth. In the last great chamber, where no one had yet painted the walls, he lowered MEme's body onto an auroch skin. With the children still leading, he dragged the skin with its terrible burden through the low narrow burrow into the secret cavern at its end.

Once they were surrounded by dancing animals, he settled MEme's body beneath bison and mammoths striding above four human handprints. He reached into her leather bandeau for her treasured piece of amber. There were still a few flecks of blood on its side. He could not imagine how they had got there. She had never conveyed to him the story of the death that allowed her family to escape. She had killed one of her father's people.

Taking the amber between his fingers, he scratched the shape of an infant's hand into the rock. He rubbed charcoal and a mixture of blood from MEme's leg and saliva from his own mouth into the grooves.

He stood up, gazed down at MEme, then kneeled again and etched another tiny hand into the stone for the infant who had died.

Finishing his work, he stretched her out, and kneeling close beside her he folded her hands across her breast and placed the amber between her clenched fingers. He drew Gleau and Ginge close and held them tightly.

"MEme," he said out loud. It was the first time he had spoken her name.

As they slipped out through the rock, their torchlight quivered and left the cavern in absolute darkness. Six handprints boldly imprinted on rock would be there two thousand generations in the future, when light next shone on the wall.

Out in the open, Plash removed his own disc of amber from its pouch and placed it inside a folded band of leather, which he wrapped around his infant daughter's tiny waist. Once she was old enough to eat solid food, he packed up their belongings and set out with his small family southward, to the home of his own people across the grasslands.

***

Eventually, kids exploring a cave in the south of France would find the amber and trade it to a traveler for a piece of silver. The traveler would sell the amber at a market stall in Paris to Thomas Jefferson, who was destined to become

The Jewel in the Cave

the American ambassador to France and third President of the United States. Jefferson would carry it across the great ocean by sailing ship to Boston, where it would be polished and given as a gift to the silversmith, Paul Revere. Revere would set it into a medallion he made for the widow of a Revolutionary leader who had recently died. The widow's name was Madge de Vere. She was a distant ancestor of the anthropologist, Angelica Harris, who discovered the exact duplicate of the amber disc buried in the dust of a secret cavern with magical paintings that would live on forever if left undisturbed.

Chapter 23

Angel sat at the kitchen table, clutching her medallion, staring at the blank television screen. Its flicker and hum were her only companions as she ate cold stew from a can. There were supplies in the cupboards to last for a year. She only intended to stay a few days. One of the cars parked in the village would need some changes, allowing her to drive without the use of her legs. Then she'd go to Paris. She had always wanted to see Paris, but her research projects had left little time for being a tourist.

There would be no one in Paris or anywhere else. She had been deep inside the earth, under a mile of limestone. Her low narrow burrow had caved in. Whatever scourge had exterminated all animal life, and her colleagues in the outer cavern, it had failed to reach her. Yet as a scientist, she suspected it wouldn't be local or regional. Death would be universal, afflicting every living creature in the entire world.

So, after Paris, where? Perhaps across the channel to London. She had no doubt she could find a boat and manage to sail it. She had sailed as a child at a camp for disabled children. She had always avoided London because of the crowds. She would find an electric wheelchair and go wherever she wanted.

She was in a surprisingly good mood, considering this was the end of the world. Her good humor made her sad. There was no one she missed.

She had friends, but none who were close enough to mourn. She was sorry about David Slocombe, but he was a colleague; they weren't close. She had no family to speak of. Her mother, Sophie, had died several years ago; her father was a stranger who lived with his new family in Vancouver. She supposed he was gone, with everyone else. Her one true friend, who had survived the plane crash with her when they were in their mid-teens, had married and had a young family before her own disabilities caught up with her and she quietly passed away. Angel remembered Maddie as the most beautiful girl in the world, although she was less than four feet tall and had a twisted back. She had blueberry eyes and a tumultuous mass of blue-black hair. She would do Angel's makeup and tell her she was beautiful too. It was Maddie who shortened Angelica's name to Angel.

Angel grieved for Maddie. She grieved for her mother, who had given her the medallion and apologized for the missing gem at its center. Sophie had not tried to explain what had happened to it. Angel grieved for the passing of all living things, but for no one else in particular.

To distract herself, she flicked through the television channels. Several showed empty newsrooms running on emergency power. Before long, they'd fade to black. She came across CNN, an American-based international broadcaster. The set was familiar. A few wisps of grey powder showed where a broadcaster had been leaning earnestly toward the camera. By the blouse crumpled across the desk and two earrings marking where her head would have been, Angel guessed who it was.

Off to the side, a large whiteboard showed a commentator's attempt to interpret breaking news using a felt marker.

The words '**Extreme Neutrino Accelerator**' were in bold print on the whiteboard, followed by arrows pointing in different directions. One arrow led to an obscured word followed by a multiplication sign and what looked like an eight on its side. Another pointed to a circle around the letters "DNA," linked to three smaller circles. The first of these contained the words "~~animal life~~," with a line drawn through them. The second said "plant life" and the third said "viruses," followed by a question mark

Then a few scribbled lines by the marker ended in a sudden stroke of black to the bottom of the board, as if pointing to a pile of clothes on the floor. The end had come in mid explanation.

Again, although Angel only occasionally watched CNN, she thought she knew who he was. Some of what he had written made sense. The eight on its side was the symbol for infinity. The multiplication sign linking it to a word she deciphered as "Hiroshima" confirmed her worst fears. Hiroshima was a city destroyed by atomic bombs in 1945. He was trying to describe a catastrophe of infinite proportions that had been caused by humans.

DNA was at the center of destruction. It is a molecular substance present in all living things with the exception of certain viruses. It basically controls identity by determining whether cells will divide and grow into a tulip or a chimpanzee. The DNA in animals and in plants is slightly different. The word animal on the board was stroked out. Anything considered "animal" was doomed and now dead.

The Jewel in the Cave

The commentator's message made it clear — whatever had happened was not the result of a natural disaster. It was not like a huge volcanic eruption clouding out the sun. Nor was it like an asteroid colliding with Earth. Such terrifying events had occurred before and would probably happen again. She realized this was a selective catastrophe — infinite, but working on an infinitesimal scale. The destruction of DNA molecules had turned all animal life into dust.

After trying the few other channels still broadcasting, Angel turned off the television and sat in the dark. Discouraged. Lonely. There was no need to understand. It wouldn't make any difference. Yet she couldn't stop thinking.

The Extreme Neutrino Accelerator was an international scientific project far different from her own research in anthropology. She had read about it and about a few scientists and religious fanatics who warned that it could be extremely dangerous. Most, however, felt that by breaking down one of the smallest particles in the universe at very high speeds they could better comprehend how life, itself, had come into existence.

As an anthropologist, her goal was much the same. No, she thought. Anthropologists explored on a human scale. They risked only their own lives in the process — especially if they searched for insight into the human condition in subterranean tunnels and secret caverns. Knowing that gave her little comfort.

She thought about science in the service of humanity. Medical discoveries were often based on destruction. Penicillin attacks bacterial infection; antibiotics attack blood poison; the Salk vaccine attacks the polio virus. But science also created the atomic bomb; the hydrogen bomb; the neutrino bomb.

Angel sighed. As far as she knew neutrino bombs had never been used, but they were able to wipe out living things while leaving inanimate objects, from boulders to buildings, intact. She had read that neutrino radiation could travel almost instantly around the world. So, it seemed that scientists at the Accelerator, who had isolated animal DNA from plant DNA, had collided neutrinos at extremely high speed and caused an explosive chain reaction. Lethal radiation was released that destroyed animate life on the planet within minutes and then, like a fog, dispersed into the atmosphere

She wondered if others had escaped. Had anyone else been locked in a chamber of rock, trapped in a coffin like the one that saved her? Would viruses survive with no one to infect? Would coral survive? It consisted of tiny animals who behaved like stone. Bees, perhaps unhatched in wax combs, deep in the hearts of giant trees? Cockroaches? Creatures in the depths of the sea? Humans? Humans who had to dig their way out from under the earth?

The thought of other living people distressed her more than the deaths of everything else. She longed for companionship, for conversation, for the sound of a voice, the touch of a hand.

In the morning, after a restless sleep, she went outside and was pleased to see the sky had brightened a little. She found an unlocked car with a full tank of gas, and some wires and duct tape, and over the next three days she fashioned hand controls with pieces from a broken rake. She managed to start the car with no problem, and drove down the road to her adopted home, where she filled the trunk with provisions.

For dinner that night, she cooked canned stew over an open fire in the fireplace. The stove didn't work. Afterward, she poured herself a glass of homemade wine. That seemed absurd, since she was in a country that produced some of the greatest wines in the world—often extremely expensive! Once in Paris, she'd try a few of the best. Dom Perignon, the world's finest champagne. Chateau Petrus, the world's most desirable red. The best sweet wine in the world, Chateau d'Yquem. They called it *sauternes.*

She didn't like wine very much, but she'd learn to.

She realized she wasn't thinking straight. There was no reaction possible that would be adequate. No thought or emotion could capture the depth of her loneliness, or the horror she felt over universal death. No words could express the terror she felt at venturing out into an empty world.

She glared at the CNN studio in Atlanta, Georgia, with the Atlantic Ocean between them. She sipped her drink. Her eyes twitched. A shift in the light; something flickered. She glowered at the screen. It was a mean joke caused by fading power.

She began to relax. There it was again. She gasped. A shadow moved across the set. In the shape of a human. She waited. The studio remained still. Hope dwindled.

Suddenly a bewildered young man shuffled in front of the whiteboard. He stopped. He walked directly toward the camera until his face filled the screen. He smiled a sad lonely smile.

Angel drew in a deep breath and smiled in return as the screen went to black. She clasped her medallion to her breast.

"My God, oh my God," she whispered. "If there are two of us, there are others." She smiled again, this time to herself.

She knew she had a very long journey ahead.

About the Author

JOHN MOSS IS THE CRITICALLY ACCLAIMED AUTHOR of the Quin and Morgan mysteries and a YA thriller, *The Girl in a Coma*. He has published more than twenty other books on Canadian culture, Arctic exploration, and experimental literature. He lives in Peterborough, Ontario, with his wife and partner, Beverley Haun, where they have been restoring an old stone farmhouse for several decades. They share their home with two terriers, Beckett and Quin, and the ghosts of Scotties long gone. **(www.johnmoss.ca)**

Made in the USA
Columbia, SC
17 May 2018